THOSE CURVES GOT ME

Amy

JUST BAE

ISBN: 978-1-925988-56-7

CONTENTS

Dr. Jack Reynold lost his mind and university hospital's research assistant, Amy Taylor was smart to send him away when he approached her after what had transpired the day before. Thoughts of what had gone right and wrong had dawned heavily on her; Jack's fingertips plucked her puffy pregnant nipples as she jerked his cock almost causing the doctor to ejaculate on her desk. They almost made out and didn't only because

Amy was called on the PA system to the first floor.

She's eight months pregnant and her verbally-abusive cocky boyfriend, Frank Ramsey works at the city's best hospital down the road. Amy and Frank have had problems since she became pregnant and Frank often leaves her for days telling her he's away for work. Amy's not innocent either; she's crossed the line with a few guys, flirting her curves and teasing but she hasn't been totally unfaithful. When she has the baby, she just wants to leave Frank.

The sensual encounter came into play that night, when Jack Reynold was in bed with his wife of fifteen years, Kate. She reached over and Jack woke up.

"Come closer, honey."

Jack came and began fondling Kate's breasts. *He really wanted her but now that she's seeing a woman as well, she wasn't his.* Jack's cock rose and Kate lifted her nightie for him to put it in her. Their ooohs and ahhhs could be heard throughout the dawn and after forty-five minutes, Jack was at the end of the bed, feeling unclean for having sex with his wife.

"You okay, honey?" Kate said, lighting up a cigarette.

"Yeah, just have a headache."

"Come here. Let me make it feel better."

Jack laid back as Kate massaged his head. They fell back to sleep until it was time for Jack to leave for work.

Jack stumbled through another day, his

mind searched for reasons why's he still with his wife. He never had thoughts about another woman until that episode with Amy. He knows that he and Kate are only together for the sake of their son Mark.

Kate started seeing one of her friends, Marlene while they were working at SmithKline and Beecham. Jack was away in Dubai for a month for a doctor's conference and Kate blamed his absence for her transgression.

Jack came home from work and took a breath before stepping inside. Mark was on the sofa, stretched out reading the book, *The Odyssey.*

"Hey, son, where's your mother?"

"She's outside, Dad," he said waving in the direction of the back.

Kate was hanging out the laundry.

"Hey, Kate."

"Jack?" Kate said jumping.

"I'm sorry. I startled you. I've been thinking—"

"Thinking about what, sweetheart?"

"About going out for dinner tonight. Just me and you. I think Mark will be okay for a few hours."

"Where?"

"Margaret's." *He overheard Amy Taylor talking about Margaret's to her colleagues at work.*

"So—you want to take me to Margaret's? What's that for?"

"Just want to spend some quality time with you—"

"I see—all right, then. Did you make the reservations yet?"

"No, I haven't."

"Well, if we want to eat tonight, I'd call them right away."

Nine o'clock was the earliest time and Jack took it. "Be a gentleman," he said as he put on his best suit seeing he hadn't shaven in weeks. Between the long hours at work, his son's soccer practices and Kate's rendezvous with her lover Marlene, Jack's probably violated his hospital's grooming protocols. *Yet, Amy likes it*, his brain remarked replaying the scene at the lab. Jack sighed forcing the memory to go away as he showered.

When he came out of the bathroom, Kate was there, arms crossed. "Out, Dr. Reynolds, my turn," she said pushing Jack out of the way.

"Okay, okay."

When they are ready to leave, they go to Mark who's playing with his Nintendo Switch in the living room.

"Son, your mother and I are heading out for dinner. I trust you won't burn the house down while we're gone." Jack said looking in the mirror. "How do I look?"

"Nice, Dad."

"Hey, put that Gameboy down and read another chapter?" Kate said.

"Mom, it's not a Gameboy. It's called—"

"Whatever it's called. Please, son, make sure you finish your reading before going to bed. We will be back late."

"Ok, Mom."

"There's some leftovers in the fridge. Just heat it up in the microwave. Okay, Mark?"

"Yes, Mom."

Kate kissed Mark on the forehead while Jack's already by the door with his coat on and glancing at the clock.

"Bye, Mom, bye, Dad!"

"Bye," Kate tossed her handbag over her shoulder and stepped outside.

"Bye, son," Jack said, "In bed by ten-ish, all right? And make sure the door's locked."

"Okay, Dad."

———

This is the first time in five years that Kate and Jack went out to dinner. Kate walked ahead of Jack as he hurried to open the car door for her but doesn't manage to do so in time. Kate got in and Jack sighed, "Can I be a gentleman for once?"

"You move too slow? Just hurry before we're late."

During the drive, Jack spent time trying to remember exactly how to go out on a date. They arrive at Margaret's and are led to their seats.

"May I take your coats?" The waiter said pulling out the chairs for them.

"Here and thank you," Jack said, slipping off his and Kate took off hers.

"Thank you!"

"You're welcome."

"Well, isn't this nice," Kate said looking around.

"Yes, it is," Jack choked, trying his hardest not to look at a woman in front of his table. *Oh my God! That's Amy Taylor! Look at those breasts coming out of her dress.* Jack hurried to open the menu almost reading every word.

"Sorry, ma'am," a man said plopping down in the seat behind Kate. It was the guy who came with Amy and Jack didn't recognize him. He looked harder and saw the hospital ID around his neck with the words, **"Frank Ramsey - Orthopaedic Surgeon"** written in bold caps on top. *What the hell is Amy doing with that foot butcher?*

"No problem—so," Kate said turning to Jack, "Did you have a good day at work? Anything new?"

"Nothing special. How about you?"

"If the house looked the same as it did when you left this morning, then you know how my day went." *Kate was bored to death working from home. She started writing contemporary romance novels three years ago and a few made the USA Today's Bestseller's list.*

At the table across them, Amy's date was blabbering about something, and Jack couldn't help but notice her looking at him every few seconds. He put his elbow on the table and rested his head in his hand so that he might do the same. *God, she's beautiful.* He began daydreaming about Kate and Dr. What's-His-Name vanishing, their tables come together and

Jack and Amy start making love on top of them.

"Jack!" Jack flinched and looked at Kate. "What are you looking at? Do I have something on my face?" Kate took out her mirror to look.

"Nothing. Just something about work. That's all."

The waiter came over to take their order after Amy and the butcher ordered first. Jack looked again seeing Amy smiling at him. The butcher snapped his fingers, getting her attention.

"Is there something on this menu that Margaret's known for, honey?" Jack said turning his eyes from Amy.

"If there was, I'd expect they'd mark it in red on the menu you were just memorizing—so you tell me?"

"Oh, I'm sorry. It's been a while since I've been out on a date."

"Well, get it together, Jack. This is my

time, honey. Not the lab rats or the girl in the red dress with the big boobs."

"Honey, what are you talking about?"

"Jack, please let's just have a good time, okay?"

"Okay, honey."

"We'll have...," Kate started saying to the waiter.

They ate, and Jack continued staring at Amy's breasts during the course of the meal. Kate noticed but didn't say anything else.

"Would you like dessert, sweetheart?"

"What time is it, Jack?"

Feels like it must be nearing midnight, Jack grumbled checking his watch, "A quarter after ten."

"No, it's all right, honey."

Suddenly, Amy stood up and started walking out with the butcher. He trailed behind her trying to pull her back. Jack then got up and told Kate he was going to the restroom.

"Ok, honey! Don't get lost."

"I won't. I'll be right back." Jack kissed Kate and headed in the bathroom's direction checking behind him to see if she was looking. Then, he snuck out spotting the surgeon and Amy's arguing.

"I don't *want* to go with you," Jack overheard Amy yelling.

"We go out to dinner and now you're not going back with me? For God's sake, I'm the father of your child."

Amy paces back and forward. "Not tonight! Leave me the hell alone!"

"Oh, now, we're playing like kids at school? Just get the hell in the car."

"No!"

The surgeon grabbed Amy and tried

dragging her into the car. Amy swung her handbag and hit him in the face. The surgeon stumbled back and Jack ran to her rescue.

"You okay, ma'am?" Jack said seeing the surgeon on the ground.

"I'm okay, Jack. Please leave."

"I'm not going anywhere."

"You hit on a pregnant woman and you think you're a tough guy, huh?"

Jack hit the man with his cane and Amy tried pulling Jack back.

"Stop it, Jack!"

The surgeon covered himself and Jack grabbed Amy's arm. Amy flinched and said, "Don't touch me, Jack."

"Amy, please—"

"Just leave me the fuck alone!" Amy gathered her things and marched back inside Margaret's.

Jack came back in and walked right by Amy who was at the mirror fixing herself. Jack's wife, Kate was sitting at the bar having a Scotch.

"Oh, you're finally back," she said. "I thought you left me. Somebody said you were fighting outside over a woman."

"Well, that's fake news!"

"Well, baby. I need you to tell you something." Kate leaned in feeling tipsy.

"What honey?"

"Sweetheart, I paid the bill so you can—"

"What?"

"Marlene's here to have a few more drinks with me."

"What the fuck? You're on a date with me, remember?"

"Jack, please not tonight. Marlene's right outside."

"Sweetheart, I told you to keep that bitch out of our lives."

"When you left me to go to Dubai to learn about taking out people's organs, I needed some attention. Remember?" Kate grabbed Jack's hand and he pulled away. "It will only be for a little while. I'll be home soon."

"Pardon me, pardon me," a woman said from behind Jack. She had on a black dress and walked right in front of him sliding onto the stool beside Kate. "Right on time, darling." Kate kissed her and put her arm around her.

"Would've been early if I could've gotten away from a minute sooner," Marlene said staring at Jack. " Oh, hi, Jack."

"Oh, Lord! You again..."

"I know, I know—don't listen to Mr. Grumpy," Kate said. "Good *night*, sweetheart. I'll see you when I get in."

"Kate, you're so fucking wrong?"

"I said I'll see you when I get home, sweetheart."

Jack walked out and thought that Amy had left but she didn't.

Two days later, Jack spotted Amy Taylor walking down the university's first-floor corridor and stopped her.

"Good morning, Amy. Will you be available to assist me in a study later this evening?" Jack asked *feeling a trickle of hope that maybe, against all reason, Amy will agree. That perhaps, afterward, she'll want to talk. They can grab a coffee and sort everything out. He can then apologize for his behavior, and explain his situation with Kate, and she will understand that his marriage is nonexistent except on paper.*

"I, I don't—"

"I'll be the guinea pig this time. I could definitely use you for this one."

"I—I don't know, Jack. You know the other night—" Amy stuttered.

"Forget about the other night. Are you free?"

"I am but not until after 8."

"Ok, I'll meet you at the lab—let's say around nine?"

"Ok."

Jack went back to his office to devise a plan on how he'll have to sneak out if Mark isn't asleep. Over the last few days, he's seen his wife only twice. She's been hanging out with Marlene in the evenings and coming home right before it's time for Mark to go to school and Jack to work.

Jack dragged through the rest of the day anticipating what happiness he can get from coming home. When he arrived, he found Mark on the couch finishing *The*

Odyssey. Jack talked about his son's favorite parts and how to tackle his book report.

At eight, Mark went upstairs and twenty minutes later, Jack left.

Jack drove to the hospital dreaming about what happened inside that room, letting the memories soothe him until when he arrived. Once he arrived, he found Dr. Rothschild in the lab instead of Amy.

"What are you—"

"I know Jack this is odd but Amy Taylor had to excuse herself this evening. She said she wasn't feeling well."

"Oh my! I hope she's going to be okay." Jack cursed under his breath.

"She'll be fine," Dr. Rothschild said bending down to wrap an Ace bandage around his ankle.

"There, that's enough," he said feeling pain.

"Would you like a magazine to take your mind off of pressure?"

"Thanks but no, thank you."

"All right. You're ready to go," Dr. Rothschild said as she left the room to turn on the machines.

"Now, Jack. You'll be put in a sort of a dream in order for us to examine actually how the mind reacts to pleasure. It's okay to express yourself," Dr. Rothschild said in the speaker in Jack's room.

"Okay, Doctor."

"Just relax. It'll only take a few minutes."

Jack lies back and tilts his head to look at the door that Amy stepped through, that night, looking ridiculous yet adorable with her wires and electrodes and oversized robe. Jack's right leg bends unconsciously and his heel presses into the hospital bed make pain creep further up his leg. He takes a few breaths and stretches it out again, then squeezes his eyes shut and reconstructs his fantasy. Amy's fingers run an inch below his navel before she removes her hand entirely. His sigh fades when she peels off her robe, treating him to the incomparable sight of her nakedness. Jack might reach for her, but she'd grab his hands. "No, no," his dream scolds him, "This is for you. Just relax." His left hand twists in the sheets, while his right plucks open his robe uncovering his cock. He uses three fingers—the best he can do to simulate. The look on Amy's face makes his cock stretch longer. Amy's first jerk is tentative and he tightens her grip with his left hand. She catches on quickly, and he's soon bucking up to meet her rhythm. His bad leg is bending, pain winding through the pleasure. Jack can't focus on stretching it back out as Amy increases the pace, can *only try to push the pain away. His apex is approaching, Jack's so close and his back is arching and Amy's name is coming out his tongue—then his foot slips, wrenching his ankle on the hospital sheets. Pain swallows pleasure and Jack bolts upright. He grips his lower leg with both hands, unable to do anything to help.*

Suddenly, the door opens and Mrs. Rothschild comes in. "Oh my, are you okay?"

"No, I'm not."

"Let me try turning up the frequency. The machine has been acting a little weird these days."

"No, I'm done. Get these damned wires off me," Jack said turning to the mirror. "Go find yourself another guinea pig, Dr. Rothschild!"

"My God, Jack! Calm down." Dr. Rothschild said as she removed the electrodes. "I think we've gotten some of the data that we need. That's the thing—even if it doesn't go as expected, there's still a sample of a result."

"What the hell are you saying?"

"I'll need you to come back for one more session at a later to complete the results."

"I'm done with this, Doctor."

"Jack, calm down, you were doing okay. What were you feeling as the machine stabilized?"

"Nothing. Are we done here, doctor?"

"Yes, Jack. You may leave. Thanks for coming."

"*Never fucking again,*" Jack said as he rushed out the door.

CHAPTER TWO

"Amy, just so you know, there's a flying pig in the bathroom."

Amy blinks away from the page she's been staring at for at least ten minutes, "What did you say, Dr. Rothschild?"

"I wanted to make sure you hadn't gone catatonic. What's going on with you?

"Frank and I, you know."

"Must have been a helluva a reason to ditch Dr. Reynolds?"

"Well, let's just say it wasn't what I

expected when I got home." Amy blushed.

"Girl, you are such a wreck."

"I know." Amy reached over to grab her coffee mug.

"Well, make sure you get some rest. The baby doesn't need to have its mother stressing out.

"Ok."

"Don't worry about anything. Frank will put a ring on that finger one of these days," Dr. Rothschild said walking away.

"I hope not," Amy murmured.

"I heard that young lady," Dr. Rothschild said surprising Amy.

Amy's baby daddy, Frank has been out of town for work for the last week and Amy since bailing out on Jack's research has been dodging him. She spotted him once walking down the corridor and hid behind a patient's room.

When she went back to her desk, she scribbled notes on one of her doctor's requests, recalling the scene when she left the restroom and saw the woman who came to meet with Jack's wife. Amy couldn't understand why Jack's wife would be with her, minutes after having dinner with him.

Amy just can't figure it out and for the rest of the days before Christmas break, kept away from that lab room. She knew better than to go there but a new fantasy sprang up; she and Jack sitting cheek-to-cheek in Margaret's bar and later ended up having sex in the restroom. Amy gasped out Jack's name as she came over and over again.

"*No! No! not again,*" Amy said getting up throughout the day and washing her privates in the bathroom.

Amy is still hamstrung over Jack but it's been now ten days since the lab episode. At dinner after a long day of returning from his travels, Amy's fiancé Frank said, "Amy? I need to talk to you about something."

Amy stared at her plate hoping for the worse. "Yes, what is it, sweetheart?"

"I'm thinking about spending the holidays with my old man before the baby comes."

"Oh, okay. Have a nice time."

"Won't you come along?" Frank said. "I'd hate to tell you but you'll have to buy your plane ticket. You know we're pinching pennies for the baby."

"No, no. Doctor's orders that us pregnant women don't fly. I'll stay put right here."

"Baby, you're only two months pregnant. You shouldn't be alone for Christmas?"

"I'll be fine, don't worry. Go see Papa and give him my regards."

"I don't want you sitting at home by yourself reading *A Christmas Carol* over and over," Frank said making Amy chuckle. "Are they still having the Christmas party at the university this year?"

"Yes, honey."

"Oh, that's fantastic! I'm sure you'll have lots of fun." Frank said being sarcastic as usual. "Who knows? You might even meet some new people there."

"I've already met all the people I work with." Amy recognized his sarcasm but didn't feel like arguing.

"Really? Everybody on the whole campus? I doubt that."

"Sweetheart, go see Papa and let me

manage this *being-at home-alone-Christmas-thing* myself. Love you."

"Love you too."

On the morning of Frank's departure, he and Amy loaded his luggage into the Uber and Frank left for the airport. Amy stayed behind and readied herself for the Christmas Party swearing to herself over and over that if Jack's there with his wife, she'll kill herself.

Tables were cleared from the middle of the university's cafeteria and red and green streamers were taped to the walls. Someone brought in a radio and set it to playing Christmas tunes that are nearly drowned out by attendees' conversations. Amy went straight for a punch bowl and poured herself a cup. The burn of alcohol makes her nauseous. She cradled the cup to her midsection and commenced looking around, trying to project an aura of poise.

As the evening goes on, Amy managed to hold a conversation or two with co-workers she was close with. In between chats, she sipped her drink finding the punch has somehow increased in alcohol. The fruit juice almost went up to her nose when she spotted Mr. Jack standing a few feet inside the cafeteria, with his suit and cane, and without Kate.

Amy can hardly believe what she's seeing. *Jack without his wife?* Powered by alcohol and indignation, Amy finished her drink and marched across the cafeteria to good ole Jack.

"Merry Christmas, Jack!"

"Thanks, Merry Christmas to you as well!"

Amy kicks herself for not thinking of something to say before she walked over here. "Your son Mark, did he find *The Odyssey*?"

"Oh yes, he finished reading it last week."

"Did he like it?"

"Very much. His favorite character was Ulysses."

Amy deeply wished she had another drink to hide behind as memories of Exam Room Five fill her unwilling mind.

"It's quite a good story. You wouldn't expect a kid from Generation Z to like something so old. Hey, who's knows? He might read *The Aeneid* next, but perhaps that would be a bit more advanced."

"Mark could benefit from the challenge."

"Oh, Mark is such a sweet boy. I remember when he came to the library," Amy slurred knowing she's talking too much.

"Thank you, he is. I don't know from whom he gets it from."

"I do."

Jack raises his eyebrows as Amy tries to figure out who said that because it couldn't possibly have been her.

"Let's dance?" Amy said steering away from the conversation.

"What did you say?"

"I said let's dance. Come on, it's Christmas."

Jack knows Amy is drunk. "I don't really—I don't dance. Can't." He lifted his cane a few inches and then let it drop.

"I think you can," Amy reached out her right hand to Jack's elbow and led him through the crowd and over to the radio.

Her hand trailed down to his and wrapped around it, lifting them up to shoulder height. Her left covered his on the cane, and she set a simple swaying rhythm that Jack falls into easily. Jack stares at her like Amy's some kind of magical being, and she can only bite her lip to temper a blinding smile. *This feels right, she knows it. No matter how wrong it is, it's still right.*

"I didn't think you'd speak to me after what I did," Jack said.

"What do you mean?"

"I scared you. I'm so sorry."

Amy shook her head, "You didn't scare me. Or, well, I was already scared. You didn't help, but you did... um, help." She closed her eyes briefly in an attempt to clear some of the haze. "You helped me not be in a position to be scared anymore."

"Regardless, I don't know what came over me."

So soon the song is ending and Jack steps away. Everything in Amy begs her not to let this become another memory she'll fantasize about. Once again, her heart takes control and words come out of her mouth, "Take me home, Jack."

"Amy..."

"I'm tired, Jack. I want to go home, I took an Uber here. I'm wasted and don't want to go alone."

"Come on, I'll drive you."

Both ignore the stares that follow them as they exit the cafeteria and walk to Jack's car. Amy's heart thuds as Jack opened the passenger door for her and she sits in. Her mind demanded to know what Amy thinks she's doing, but she has no answer for it. She just sat there and tried not to stare at Jack for more than three seconds at a time while she gave him directions. Jack Reynold's such a mystery to her, for all that she feels like she knows him so well. "May I ask what happened to your leg?" Amy sighed, "I mean, um, it's fine if you don't want to talk about it."

"I was drafted in '04," Jack said, his eyes fixed on the road. "So, I went to basic training, and...well, then..."

"An accident?"

"No. No, there wasn't an accident. I got a call from my wife and she told me she was pregnant. At that moment... nothing else mattered. The only thing that mattered was that I came straight home. My father abandoned me when I was lit-tle. I couldn't—I could never do that to my son. *Nothing* would make me do that. Even if it meant...so, I left the office where soldiers took calls from outside, and kept walking, and didn't stop until a jeep ran over my foot."

"Oh my God, Jack!"

"I was discharged in hours, of course. Most of the bones healed, but not all. Now you know." He glanced over at her.

"Well, Mark has his father. Turn here, it's the second house on the right."

Jack parked and then opened the passenger door for Amy. They walked to her house and Amy's feeling woozy. "At Margaret's, was the woman you were with, your wife?"

"Yes."

"But—I saw her with someone else."

"Well, yeah. Kate's lover means more to her than I do."

Amy stopped watching Jack languish. Her mind is blank when she stepped forward and wrapped her hand around the back of Jack's head. His mouth landed on hers.

The kiss was only for a moment, then Jack pulled away. "I'm sorry," he gasped.

Amy can hardly hear him through the blood pounding in her veins. Jack's lips are parted and wet, and all Amy does is smile.

"I'm not sorry," Amy said, closing the distance between them.

Amy clung to Jack's head and shoulder as the heat roared through her, stroking her tongue over his and scraping his lower lip with her teeth when he retreats. A growl rolled from his throat into her mouth and Jack kissed her harder. Amy's nails dig deep into his scalp and coat causing them to stumble. Her back hit the wall beside the front door.

"Wow!"

"I'm yours," Amy said, her voice low and desperate, "You know that, don't you?"

"I do."

Amy moaned and her leg has loosely hooked itself over Jack's and she pressed up against him in a way she's only done in her most fevered fantasies. She'd rather die than stop, realizing with something between elation and panic that they don't have to. Her boyfriend, Frank is likely halfway to Maine right now and the house is empty. Amy can pull Jack inside and finally take what she wanted for a long time.

She wanted to get to the door first, and can't make herself loosen her grip on Jack. She managed to inch closer to it, but then he ducked his head and started sucking on her neck. Her arm dropped and elbow hit the doorbell, sending a chime through the empty row home. A second later, lights came on inside.

"Christ!" Amy hollered and shoved Jack away.

Jack blinked, looking up at the windows, "Who's that?"

"Bloody Frank, I thought he was gone!" Amy said.

"Damn it," Jack moved back, but Amy grabbed his hand and pulled him closer.

"There's a hotel. Hollytree, on Stanmore. Meet me there tomorrow night at ten o'clock."

"Are you sure?"

"I am. Now, hurry."

"I'll be there." He stole one last kiss, then spun around, scooped his cane off the ground, and hurried to his car.

Amy put her hand over her mouth and grabbed her key and opened the door, Frank was dressed in a housecoat standing on the stairs.

"Amy, there you are, sweetheart. Would you believe it? There was engine trouble on the plane, so my flight was canceled until tomorrow. Hey, why did you ring the doorbell?"

"My elbow slipped, good night," Amy said bolting up the stairs and into the bathroom.

Oh my God! she whispered sitting on the toilet. *I almost got caught. Shit!*

CHAPTER THREE

Jack dragged his feet through the extra shift he took at the hospital, lost in a haze, unable to come to terms what would happen tonight. He called Mark to tell him that he would be home soon and asked where his mother was. Mark told him that she wasn't there and Jack told him to do his homework.

The day's end comes, and Jack comes home finding Mark sitting on the sofa as he enters. "Hello, son."

"Hi, Dad."

Jack hung up his coat and look at Mark. For the first time in weeks, he doesn't have a book in his hands. Instead, he's rigid and hunched over, looking at the carpet. "Is something wrong, son?"

Mark looked up. "Mom didn't come home today. She always does, after school. Where is she? I'm hungry."

Jack crossed the room and put his hand on Mark's shoulder. "It'll be okay, son. She'll be here soon." he said, "Just... just wait here one minute. I'll be right back."

Jack went to their bedroom and checked the closet and the drawers. There was a complete absence of anything belonging to her. Jack looked around and spotted a corner of something white tucked beneath the pillow on the bed. He pulled out a piece of paper. *"I'm not coming back. Take care of Mark."* It's all

Jack needed to hear and it wasn't something he hadn't been expecting. He folded the paper and walked back downstairs to Mark. He put his arm around his son and said, "Mark, your mother's not coming home."

"Why?"

Jack took out the letter from his pocket. "Your mother wrote this. You can read it if you like. I can tell she was unhappy here and needs to find her own way."

"Without us?"

Jack squeezed his son as tight as he can. "So it would seem, son. But, I'll never leave you, Mark. You'll always have me. I promise."

Mark sobbed and is shaken, curling up against his father. Jack nearly felt a measure of peace as he comforted his son.

Jack cooked Mark supper, and afterward put him to bed like he hasn't since Mark hit double digits. Stretched out, Jack read aloud from *The Aeneid*, thinking of Amy. He looked at the clock seeing it's near ten.

"Keep reading Dad," Mark said.

Mark cried, and Jack cradled him until the boy finally fell asleep.

Jack slowly got up from the bed and close the door behind him. He stood for a few moments in the dark hallway, wavering between staying and heading out the front door. Jack ultimately grabbed his coat and car keys and headed out.

It's not until Jack's parked that he realizes he has no idea what room Amy is in. He got out and stood beneath one of the parking lot's lamps, staring at two rows of hotel doors. In luck, a curtain twitched aside, and one of the doors opened. Amy walked out onto the upper deck and Jack spotted her. "May I come up?"

Jack thought Amy nodded before she went back inside. He climbed a flight of stairs and followed the lights leading to her hotel room. Jack went inside seeing Amy standing with her arms over her stomach.

"I meant to—" he stuttered wanting to say, "call." Instead, Jack continued, "My wife just left me."

"What?"

"She's gone along with her clothes."

"Did she take your son?"

"No, no, she-ah. No, Mark's home asleep."

"I'm so sorry."

Jack blinked and truly looked at Amy for the first time since entering the room. She looked back at him, leaving only pure empathy.

"She fucking left him," Jack said, as his eyes began tearing. Amy pulls him inside and sat him on the creaky mattress.

"I'm so sorry, Jack."

"I thought you said you weren't sorry."

"I did, and I'm not. That's my dilemma."

"I don't want you to be. Not for any of this."

Jack leans on Amy's shoulder looks up at her. "Tell me what to do, Amy. I'm so lost."

"Well, go home and be with your son. He's had his world fall apart and he needs you."

Jack nodded.

"Call me up when you're ready, Jack."

"What about you?"

"I'll be sitting here alone with a child soon."

"What are you saying?"

"Yes, that's why I'm here with you tonight. Frank left me for some huzzy at the hospital. They're transferring to Singapore at the end of the month. What a deadbeat?"

"I'm so sorry."

"Don't be. I'll be okay."

Their faces are close, and Jack wanted to kiss her, but he limited himself to pressing his lips on her cheek. He lingered there as Amy's arms tighten around him. When he pulled away, she released him.

"Let me drive you home?"

"All right."

Amy gathered her things and canceled her reservation for the night.

Jack can't stop looking at Amy as they drive to her place. When they pull up in front of her house, he couldn't resist the urge to reach for her hand and bring it to his lips. He kisses her fingers and began sucking the tips. But Amy pulled her hand back, instead of kissing and licking Jack's.

"This is for you, sweetheart until later," Amy said moving her tongue up and down each finger. Her eyes stay fixed on him and she said, "Later."

"Later."

She got out of the car and walked to her house. Jack didn't block until she was inside. He pulled off, happy that they didn't make another mistake.

CHAPTER FOUR

The next few weeks go by without Jack's wife Kate coming by at least to check on Mark. Her lawyer sent the divorce papers in the mall making Jack grieve inside. He signed them and days later, their marriage was dissolved. To take his mind off the pain, he spent more time with Mark, going out to dinner when he got off and buying Mark whatever he wanted.

Amy went into labor and Jack heard about it in the middle of a patient's checkup. He wanted to ring up Amy to find out how she was doing but doesn't. He just walk to where Amy's normally stationed to just say hi to her fill-in.

That evening, Jack gave in and told himself he would sit down with Mark to discuss him seeing another woman.

"Who?" Mark asked after his father opened the discussion at dinner.

"Do you remember I told you about the woman at the hospital's library?"

"The one who told you about *The Odyssey*?"

"Yes."

"Oh, yeah, she's nice."

"You think so?"

"Yeah, so, you want to take her out, huh? Wasn't she pregnant?"

"Yes, she was. She had the baby and now is at home resting. I hope this doesn't make make you feel uncomfortable."

"Well, I won't know unless you do it."

"Fair enough, so."

Amy called Jack at work a week after her delivery and told him to come by after work. Jack felt like a teenager again, the first time he came inside her home withstanding the looks and questioning faces of her neighbors wondering about *Amy Taylor and Mr. Frank Ramsey.*

Amy said, "Good night!" to her babysitter as she grabbed Jack's arm and marched with him out the front door.

And that was the first of a few dates, all scheduled while Amy was on her first month of maternity leave.

A month into their courtship, Jack found himself in a jewelry store in town, inspecting the best ring his budget would allow. A little voice crawled around the back of his mind whispering, *you think Amy would marry me.* Jack doesn't listen and buys the ring. It lives in his suit pocket and the small velvet box becomes dusty during each date. He almost crushed it when Amy suggested for their next date that they go to Margaret's.

"Really? You want to go there?"

"I'm sure we'll be fine. We don't expect Frank or what's her name to be there. Do we?"

"No."

And indeed, they enjoyed one of the best dinners Jack can remember before venturing to the bar. He wondered if he should be uncomfortable, but the memory of Kate with Marlene withered away as he watched Amy sip from a glass of wine. Her gaze lit on him only to jump away, and he noticed her cheeks slowly turned a shade not far distant from her drink.

"I feel as if I've missed the joke," he said.

"Not so," she said with her chin almost touching her chest.

Jack leaned in closer. "What then?"

Amy leaned in closer until they're almost cheek-to-cheek. "I had this fantasy about us, being here... then going into the restroom together and, um..."

Jack saw his cock rising and tried patting it down, "I see." Images race through his mind of Amy's dress hiked up over her hips, her hands holding his shoulders while he grabs her thighs and pounds into her. She screamed "Jack, Jack" every ten seconds.

"Anyway, we're not doing that. Just a thought. I'm still recovering, you know."

"Oh, we're not."

"Not unless we—"

"No, until we are—" Amy stopped talking and so did Jack. Her face is unreadable as she looked at him, but Jack found his fingers wandering into his pocket anyway while his heart hammered in his chest.

"Amy?"

"Yes?"

"I love you. I'll never love anyone the way I do with you. I know it hasn't been long, and nothing has to change right away, we can carry on like this as long as you like, but..." Jack opened the box and held it up. "Please tell me you'll marry me."

Amy only stared at him. Then, her head went up and down. "I will."

"You will?"

"Yes."

"Oh, my God!"

Somewhere far away, the bar's patrons applaud and the bartender announced, "Free champagne for the happy newlywed, and glasses all around!"

Amy and Jack broke apart to smile to the bartender and anyone who came up to pat their backs and wish them the best.

Jack gently wipes a tear away with his thumb. "Thank you. I love you."

"I love you too, Jack," Amy said. They kissed again before having another few drinks and leaving the restaurant.

Jack dropped Amy off but declined to go inside. On the drive home, he envisioned the way he'll break the news to Mark tomorrow, hoping he'll take it well.

He climbed in bed, letting Amy's wonderful fantasy play out in his mind. A few tugs and Jack sat up groaning. He then masturbated saying her name until he finally became tired.

CHAPTER FIVE

Amy's postpartum period was over and she and Jack started going over each other houses daily but never had sex. This evening, Jack told Amy he'll cook dinner before they head out to their clinical appointment with Dr. Rothschild.

Amy convinced Jack to go back for the second part of his experiment, telling him that she had volunteered after Dr. Rothschild had contacted her. Dr. Rothschild explained that she was seeking to explore differences between a coupling who is close to marrying and have one child from a previous relationship. The condition was that both parties never had sex prior. *How convenient!* Dr. Rothschild gave her a date and time and they ultimately both agreed to participate.

Amy was on the couch while Mark was reading.

"That dragon kind of came out of nowhere," Mark said to Amy closing the book.

"I think they wanted Beowulf to go out with a bang."

Amy loved to continue discussing this with Mark, but found her eyes constantly roaming to the clock. It was getting late and their appointment was scheduled for 11 PM. She looked over in Jack's direction seeing him washing dishes. Mark had started yawning and finally told them he's going to bed.

"See ya!" Amy said.

"See ya! Thanks, Amy."

"You bet."

Amy sat upright, hearing Mark leave the bathroom to his bedroom. "I think we're all clear," she whispered grinning.

"Ok, I'm ready. I hope this goes better than the last time," Jack said.

"I'm sure it will, sweetheart."

"It was so weird being in that chair so sucked into subspace."

"Hmm, it sounds freaky."

"Well, it was, especially for an old man like myself."

"You're not old, Jack. Stop it!"

As they went to the closet, Jack grabbed both of their coats and put on Amy's first.

Amy hummed along on the way to the hospital texting her babysitter to make sure her newborn was okay. Her hand and Jack's found each other in the car's dark interior, drifting and lacing each other's tightly.

Within thirty minutes, they arrived at Exam Room Five in the university's clinical studies wing. It was difficult for them to keep their eyes off each other as they got undressed. Once they put on their robes, Dr. Rothschild came out and greeted them. "Jack, whatever you do. Let Amy have satisfaction first, please," Dr. Rothschild said handing them their electrodes, condoms, and earpieces.

"Ok, Dr. Rothschild. But I'm warning you she's the curviest woman I've ever been with."

"Jack, you'll be fine. Just keep that in mind."

"Jack, you listen to the doctor, okay?"

"Haha, very funny!"

Dr. Rothschild went on to tell the couple that she was monitoring the signals but couldn't actually see the experiment. It was the hospital's policy. They signed off on the final waiver and Dr. Rothschild left telling them to relax and have fun.

Jack sat at the end of the bed in a blue bathrobe twitched aside exposing his injured ankle. Amy opened the bag she'd brought from home and pulled out a towel, wrapping it around his lower leg. She then took a medium-sized collar and buckled it over the towel. "There," she said, "No rough stuff buddy."

"Who says no?"

Amy stood up and brought her hands down to the belt of her robe. "I did. Now watch me undress," Amy said as she untied the belt and let her robe slip down off her shoulders.

"Oh my! Those curves."

Amy's body was curvier now that she had the baby. Her breasts were milky and she felt vindicated. At this moment, all she thought about was her baby daddy Frank complaining about how curvy she was but he was long gone.

"Meanwhile, you can put your hands underneath and see what you can find that's wet."

"Is this part of the experiment?"

"Mic-check—I hear you guys in there," Dr. Rothschild said in the earpieces.

"Can we have some privacy, Doctor?" Jack said.

"Yes, Jack. You already do. I won't see what's happening. Now continue on."

Amy's robe hit the floor and she didn't wait for another second to let her hands dive inside Jack's robe, rubbing his chest and downward. "Oh my, Jack! What do you have here, buddy?"

Jack's hands met Amy's thighs and ran up over her hips to her waist, gently tugging until Amy straddled him. Once on top, Jack sucked her nipples, causing her to moan *'Jack '*as the breastmilk flooded his mouth. "I've done something right if I hear you say that."

Amy giggled, "And I know what makes that thing down there so hard."

Jack chuckled, "And what's that?"

Amy wrapped her hand around the back of his neck while the other went to his cock. One jerk made Jack hiss as his eyelids fluttered.

"God, Amy," he gasped leaning up to kiss her, managing to avoid the electrodes as he continued sucking her breast filling his mouth with milk. Amy continued jerking and Jack felt he was about to ejaculate.

"Jack, do something that'll raise your heart rate a little," Jack heard Dr. Rothschild say in his earpiece. Amy heard it as well.

"But, Doctor..."

"Do it now before the meter goes too low."

"Fuck me now, Jack. Suck the milk out of my titties," Amy begged, "Oh, Jack!"

Amy rose on her knees high enough to position Jack where she needed him. She lowered, breathing through the pressure of him entering. She's been thinking about this all day and can't wait any longer.

Jack's hands slid down to her curvy ass and he squeezed.

"That's it, right there, Jack," Amy moaned. She closed her eyes again and laid her head in the hollow between Jack's shoulder and neck as she surrendered to the pleasure. She started off slow but soon sped up until her head rocked back. Jack's mouth descended on her neck, seeking out her G spots. The pleasure crested through Amy, leaving her gasping for more.

When her heartbeat slows, Dr. Rothschild, said in their earpieces, "Amy, I need you to raise your heart rate?"

"Ok, Doc."

"Oh God, Jack! Fuck me, fuck me." Her muscles tighten as Jack stroked harder.

"Fuck me faster, faster...ah, ah, ah, Oh my God!!!!!!!" Amy said knowing Dr. Rothschild was likely listening in on them. She gazed in the mirrored glass as Jack kept thrusting. "Oh, he's so wonderful, Doctor," she gasped. Jack's eyes were shut, his hands were holding Amy steady for his erratic thrusts, which Amy matched by tightening her grip on his ass.

"Yes, yes, oh God! That's it, Jack. Right there, right there."

"Ah- Amy!" Jack squeezed Amy, squirming. Unfortunately, he was the one who came first.

"Jack, why's your heart rate going down? Please raise it," Dr. Rothschild said through the earpiece.

"He came, Doctor. Jack broke the rules."

"Shit, shit, shit! I'm sorry, Doctor. I told you those curves..."

"Experiment's over. We'll have to go off the data we have. Thanks a lot, Jack."

Amy eased off Jack and soon Dr. Rothschild appeared to help them unplug. Amy unbuckled the collars from Jack's leg and unwrapped the towel before gently lowering his leg to the floor.

"Did we actually contribute something to science, Dr. Rothschild?" Jack said visibly embarrassed.

"I'd say, "Yes, Jack." The full readings were almost in. I think we have enough data to go off of though. I wouldn't be surprised if these were published in next month's journal. Anonymously, of course."

"How exciting!" Amy said hugging Jack.

"You are good for each other. Best of wishes to you in your upcoming marriage!"

"Thank you, Doctor."

"I'm sure there are couples around the world who wish they had your bond. Though I don't know how many would do a test like you. It seems like a one-in-a-million odds."

"Yeah, Doctor. I have to train good ole

Jack here how to maneuver these curves of mine."

"Thanks for participating, guys and see you around," Dr. Rothschild said walking out of the room.

Amy and Jack finished dressing and returned to their car. She grabbed Jack's hand and presses the back of it to her cheek as they drive home through the night.

"Those curves got me," Jack said turning on the radio.

"I know. You ain't the first one to say that."

ACKNOWLEDGMENTS

Thanks for reading and please leave a review. This will really help us out.

Consider joining our mailing list by sending us a hi at therealjustbae@gmail.com. We give out FREE Audiobook codes all the time.

Join our IG page here: instagram.com/justbaebooks

Join our FB page here:
facebook.com/authorjustbae

Best of regards,
Just Bae